HarperCollins®, ✿®, HarperFestival®, and Festival Readers™
are trademarks of HarperCollins Publishers Inc.

Harold and the Purple Crayon: Harold Finds a Friend
Text copyright © 2002 by Adelaide Productions, Inc.
Illustrations copyright © 2002 by Adelaide Productions, Inc.
Printed in the U.S.A. All rights reserved.
Library of Congress Catalog Card number: 2001095573
www.harperchildrens.com

1 2 3 4 5 6 7 8 9 10

✣

First Edition

HAROLD and the PURPLE CRAYON™

Harold Finds a Friend

Text by Liza Baker
Based on a teleplay by Carin Greenberg Baker
Illustrations by Kevin Murawski

HarperFestival®
A Division of HarperCollinsPublishers

Harold couldn't sleep.

He wanted to play, but he had
no one to play with.

He decided to play
with his stuffed dog, Lilac.
He threw a rubber ball
across the room.

Lilac didn't chase the ball.

Lilac didn't bring the ball back.

She couldn't.

Lilac was just a stuffed animal.

Harold wanted a real dog,
so he picked up his purple crayon
and set off on an adventure.

Harold drew a path and
started on his way.

He drew a rubber ball.

It was perfect for playing catch.

Harold threw the ball,

and it bounced away.

Lilac caught the ball.

She brought it to Harold.

Harold tossed the ball again.

Once more, Lilac chased after it.

At last, Harold had a dog who

liked to play catch.

Lilac was good at tricks, too.

A dog who does tricks deserves a

reward, so Harold drew a big box

of dog biscuits.

After each trick,

Harold gave Lilac a biscuit.

"Good dog," he said.

But Lilac was impatient.

She jumped onto Harold's lap.

She grabbed the box of biscuits

and started digging a hole.

Lilac was trying to bury the box.
She kicked dirt into the air and
covered Harold from head to toe.

Harold told Lilac to stop.

She looked sad.

Her feelings were hurt.

Lilac ran away.

18

Harold was alone again.

He decided to wait for Lilac

to come back.

He was tired, so he drew a chair.

Harold waited for a long time.

He grew bored.

Then he had an idea.

He'd draw a new friend.

Harold drew a large round bowl.

Then he drew a plump goldfish.

But the fish didn't want to play.

It just swam in circles.

So Harold drew a big dog.

The dog sat down, rolled over,

and fell asleep.

A sleeping dog isn't any fun,

thought Harold.

Harold drew a very peppy dog.

Harold drew a ball and threw it.

But instead of bringing it back,

the dog played with the ball

all by itself.

This dog was no fun.

Lilac was a good friend,

even when she misbehaved.

Harold had to find her,

so he drew a lighthouse.

He climbed the stairs

to the highest point.

He followed the path of the light

and looked in every direction.

Finally, he spotted Lilac.

Harold rushed to Lilac.

Harold patted her happily.

Lilac wagged her tail.

She was happy, too.

Harold drew another ball.

He threw it for Lilac again and again

until they were tired.

Harold and Lilac rested.

Then it was time to go home.

Harold reached up and drew his
bedroom window around the moon.

Harold was back in his bedroom.

Harold slipped into bed.

He was happy to be home with

his good friend Lilac.

As he curled up with Lilac,

Harold's purple crayon dropped

to the floor.

And he dropped off to sleep.